The Adventures of Jimini and Jacko

The Smarty Boys

By Maureen Cotter

Illustrations by Hafsa Pinar

Print ISBN: 979-8-35091-847-2

Printed in the United States of America

Maureen Cotter originally penned these stories for her two young grandsons,
who made several trips to Wales from their Australian home.
Born and brought up in the Rhondda Valley, Maureen continues to live
in South Wales and is now planning a sequel.

She is an expert at baking Welshcakes!

For James and Lachlan,
with fondest love

CONTENTS

1

MISCHIEF ON THE FARM

This is the story of Jimini and his brother Jacko, the Smarty Boys. It's about the day they decided to make mischief on the farm beside Pen Onn Cottage, in deepest Wales – or Cymru, as it's known, in Welsh. Are you sitting comfortably? Then I'll begin.

Perhaps you are wondering first of all how the boys got to the small village of Pen Onn? Well, they arrived in a rocket, which had been launched from their front garden in Australia. Their Dad built the rocket in his garage with a big set of tools. He made all the calculations and checked everything on his computer so that the rocket would be perfect.

Jimini and Jacko arrived at Pen Onn Cottage in the dead of night and frightened Nanny and Grampy to death by knocking on the bedroom window and calling to come in. When Nanny opened the window she recognised them straight away and went straight into the kitchen to make them a midnight snack of sausages and pickle on brown bread.

Then Grampy found them a box to snuggle up in till morning, when it could be decided what to do with them. The rocket had landed in the back garden and the horses in the field next door were staring at it in amazement. Next door's cat was spitting at it, but their dog just walked over calmly and weed on the side of it!

Grampy decided to put the rocket in the garage so it would be out of the way till it was needed again. Jimini and Jacko asked Nanny if she would make them some Welshcakes, as their Mum had told them all about Nanny's Welshcakes when they were in Australia.

After breakfast the next day, the two boys were eager to look around. When they learned there was a farm nearby they whispered to one another that here was the chance to have an adventure.

Up to the farm they went and walked straight into the lambing shed. At this time of year, the mother sheep were just having their lambs and several had been born that very day. The dear little creatures were wobbling about on their weak little legs and bleating for milk from their mums. Jimini and Jacko decided it would be fun to have a ride on the back of a lamb, just like you would ride a pony. So they clambered on the backs of two black and white lambs that looked a bit bigger than the rest.

Jacko called out "Hey, let's have a race!" So the two Smarty Boys gave their lambs a poke in their bellies and the little black-legged lambs started to tear around the lambing shed. At that moment the farmer's wife walked in and stood rooted to the spot. She thought the two lambs must have eaten something that didn't agree with them and called out to her husband "Come quickly – the lambs have gone mad!"

Just then the farmer rushed in with his gun, because they sometimes shoot mad animals. Luckily Grampy arrived at that moment too. Jimini and Jacko jumped off quickly and the lambs stopped careering around and started behaving quite normally again. The farmer thought the lambs must have been having a bit of fun, so he just gave them a pat on the head and shooed them away.

But what of the two boys who had caused all the trouble? Well, when the Smarty Boys jumped off the lambs' backs they had jumped straight into a heap of manure, and disappeared into it. In the middle of the heap was a great big worm who didn't like being disturbed. So he lashed his tail and threw them even deeper into the pile.

Jacko began to cry as he hated the smell, and then Jimini started to cry because some had got into his mouth and it tasted horrid. All of a sudden a big beetle loomed up in front of them and said sternly "Get out of my way! Or I'll feed you to my babies, who are very hungry."

The very thought of being fed to the baby beetles made the Smarty Boys move pretty fast. They took one big leap, shot out of the manure and landed in a puddle of water. They washed themselves down as best they could and scooted back to Nanny's house as fast as their little legs would carry them.

Nanny was very cross and only gave them raw potato for their supper and sent them to bed early. They were actually quite glad to get into bed and feel safe and sound again, so they dropped off to sleep quite quickly and slept soundly until the next morning. And that's the first adventure they had in the village of Pen Onn. Which means "head of the hill," by the way, in Welsh.

2
DOWN THE PLUGHOLE

The day after the Smarty Boys had played havoc at the farm, Nanny got them up early and said "You two need a good bubble bath. We need to save hot water, so you'd better get in the bath straight after me."

The boys were afraid to argue, so they hopped in after Nanny and really enjoyed splashing around and hiding under the bubbles and making them go pop. But pretty soon they were looking for something else to do and Jacko whispered "I know, let's pull the plug out and give Nanny a shock."

They heaved away until they managed to pull the plug right out, but they didn't realise that the water goes down the plughole with quite a force, and before they knew it there was a big *Swoosh* and they had both gone down with all the soapy water. Nanny felt the water draining out and tried desperately to put the plug back in and save the boys, but they were gone! And there was nothing she could do. You wouldn't expect her to run out into the courtyard and start picking up the manhole covers in her nightie, would you? She would have given the milkman a fright or worse things could have happened to her.

So, just what happened to Jimini and Jacko in the meantime? Well, they soon found themselves down in the sewers near Pen Onn. "Now what a pretty mess you've got us into," said Jimini. They managed to clamber on to a fairly wide ledge running down either side of the pipe. There, they sat down to work out what to do next. They were lost. They didn't want to end up nearly up to their eyes in you-know-what. And they were hungry and longing to be back in Penn Onn Cottage eating Nanny's Welshcakes.

Suddenly Jacko said "Don't move Jimini, but I'm sure I can hear someone breathing quite near us." They kept quite still. They were now used to the dark and could see quite well. They turned slowly and concentrated their eyes on a corner just behind them. And sure enough, there *was* someone there – for they could see two glistening eyes staring at them.

"Whoooo issss there?" they asked, with their little hearts pumping away like mad. After a moment's silence a gruff voice replied "I'm Stumpy, one of the sewer rats." He sounded quite friendly, so the boys edged nearer until out of the shadows came a big brown, wet rat. The sad thing about him was that he was crying big ploppy tears.

"What's wrong?" asked the boys. Stumpy explained "I was born without a tail, and all the other rats won't have anything to do with me. They shoo me away when I try to play with them, and even splash me with poo, and sometimes they even throw things at me to make me go away. So I have to live on my own, and I don't even know if my mother misses me. *And* I'm called Stumpy!" The rat broke down in uncontrollable tears at this point, which made Jacko cry too. Well, he was the youngest Smarty Boy and he usually cried most.

Jimini decided that he'd have to take control of the situation, and with a voice of authority he said "Now, you two, stop this howling. Get yourselves together. We are going to plan a campaign so Stumpy can hold his head up and become Boss Rat." Jimini wasn't sure what he really meant by that but he had to think fast because Stumpy was looking at him in amazement and was wiping his eyes with the back of his paw.

"Now, let me see," said Jimini. "I know – collect together all the bits and bobs you can see around and make three enormous heaps of them." "What sort of things?" asked Stumpy. "We want things that are going to make suitable ammunition like bottle tops, pebbles, and coins," replied Jacko. "In fact anything that gets lost down drains, but isn't too big."

In next to no time they had a huge pile of all manner of things, and they even found a cat's collar that had slipped down the drains from somewhere or other. "Come here Stumpy," said Jimini. "I'm going to put this collar around your neck to make you look very important. Now, divide the spoils into three heaps. Then we'll hide behind these crevices in the sewer pipes and wait until the other rats come along to torment you, Stumpy."

"They usually come after lunch," said Stumpy. "When they're full up with food they don't know what to do with themselves, so they think it's fun to come up here and call me names." Suddenly, in the distance the three friends could hear the rats chanting their favourite song. And this is how it went:

"Fi Fo Fat

You're a silly old rat

You have no tail

And a nose like a nail

You should be in jail

Fi Fo Fat."

Stumpy began to cry again, and great big tears plopped down on the ground around his feet. "None of that," said Jimini. "When those rats come in sight, and I give the word, we'll bombard them with our ammunition."

The chanting came closer and closer. Then the rats came in sight, laughing and singing and enjoying their big joke. "Fire!" shouted Jimini, and together the three friends hurled their ammunition. The rats were completely taken by surprise, and of course they thought only Stumpy was there. The first rat was knocked sideways and had to be carried off. The next two rats were hit on their noses and ran off yelping. Then the rats behind them who were not really sure what was happening found themselves being pelted with bottle tops, pebbles and gravel.

At this point, Stumpy was pushed forward by Jimini and Jacko. He was a bit nervous, but he felt so important with his cat's collar on. He stood on his hind legs as tall as he possibly could and spoke in a deep, booming voice. Jimini had quickly written him a speech and this is what he said. "I am a rat without a tail. That makes me different from any other rat in this sewer. I was born to be KING Stumpy, and from now on you will all take your orders from me and treat me with respect. Do you understand?"

To Stumpy's amazement all the sewer rats lay down flat on their tummies and said altogether "You are indeed our king. Please forgive our sins of the past. We are now your servants." Stumpy replied "Go home and prepare a feast for me and a comfortable bed. I shall be there in ten minutes."

The rats picked themselves up, bowed to Stumpy and then scurried away. Stumpy turned to the Smarty Boys. "How can I ever thank you?" he asked. "Well, first get us back to Pen Onn," said Jimini. Stumpy knew all the secret passages leading out of the sewer and soon had them back in the garden of Pen Onn Cottage. Nanny was hanging out her washing, thinking that the Smarty Boys were gone forever. She screamed when she saw Stumpy and jumped up on the wall!

Jimini and Jacko soon explained who Stumpy was and Nanny was glad to hear that the boys had been able to help someone in distress. She smiled at Stumpy and said he could come back to Pen Onn whenever he wished. Stumpy said goodbye to the boys and scooted off. "But I've got a feeling he'll be back one of these days," smiled Nanny as she went to fetch the tired, hungry Smarty Boys a fresh plate of Welshcakes.

3

OFF TO BIG PIT

Today was Tuesday. The refuse men had been and the Smarty Boys had watched the rubbish being thrown into the lorry. Then they'd watched Grampy mend some fuses with his drill and handsaw. They had also seen Nanny make Knickerbocker Glories in the kitchen for lunch. Then they were at a bit of a loose end. "Can't we go somewhere in the car, Nanny?" asked Jacko.

"Well, let me see… how would you boys like to go to Big Pit?" said Nanny. "Whatever is that?" asked Jimini.

"Well, I expect you know that coal comes from under the ground," replied Nanny. "It's cut away from the rocks underground by the coal miners. Then they load it into trucks, which are brought up to the surface in a pit cage. When the coal is at the top, other miners clean it up – which means sorting it out into good coal and useless pieces that won't burn and are thrown away.

"The good coal is then loaded into bags and trucks and delivered to houses and factories for fires or electricity. As a matter of fact," Nanny continued, "my father *was* a coal miner, and once when he was working underground a huge boulder fell on his head and made him completely deaf. Mining can be a very dangerous job and most people wouldn't want to be miners."

The boys were listening earnestly. "We're talking about Big Pit however," Nanny continued. "This pit is no longer used for actual coal mining, but is kept as a showpiece museum, where visitors can go underground and see what it was like there. It gives them a good idea of how hard it can be working eight hours without any sight of daylight."

The boys nodded. "Years ago," Nanny continued, "before the coal trucks underground were motorised, they were pulled along the track by pit ponies. These poor ponies were taken underground when they were quite young and never came to the surface again. However, they usually had two or three people whose special job it was to look after the pit ponies and they were as kind as possible to them, trying not to work them too hard and feeding them regularly. My grandfather was in charge of the pit ponies and he loved them, but felt very sorry for them too, especially when he had to leave them at the end of his shift underground."

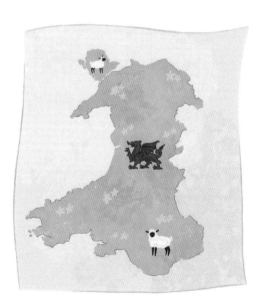

Nanny paused for breath and Jimini and Jacko both said at once "Oh please Nanny, take us to Big Pit!" So a picnic bag was packed, the car filled with petrol and they were off. Big Pit is in a place called Blaenavon, and young children are allowed to go underground there with their parents.

Once they arrived, Nanny and Grampy had to pay for tickets and get special hard hats to wear underground in case someone got a bump on the head. Of course, there were no hard hats small enough for the Smarty Boys but Nanny had thought of this before leaving Pen Onn and had made quite good hats out of the tops of bottles. They were lined with wool to give a cosy fit.

Actually they looked quite funny and as soon as Jimini and Jacko looked at each other, they rolled over on the ground laughing. "Please stop or I'll split my skin!" pleaded Jacko. He thought for a moment and added, "or perhaps I'll die!" Everyone stopped laughing straight away but it was even funnier when Nanny said they also had to wear specially big boots in case something dropped on their feet.

Soon they were all inside Big Pit and ready to go down in the pit cage. What an odd sensation that was! On the way down, the Smarty Boys made friends with two ordinary little boys who didn't think it was a bit odd to see and hear the two tiny Smartys talking quite normally.

When the cage reached the bottom, the two little boys, whose names were Jim and Basil, ran off without telling anyone where they were going. This was against the rules of course, but some little boys never do what they are told.

The rest of the party followed their guide carefully and did exactly what they should. Now and again everyone had to crawl on all fours under low rocks. This was hard on your knees, and Jacko had to have a plaster on one of his. They saw the old pony stables – no ponies there now of course – and the old trucks into which the coal used to be loaded. Here and there water dripped from the roof of the tunnels and they could only see in the darkness with the beam of light from the lamps fixed to the front of their helmets.

At last the tour was over and everyone was told to line up in front of the pit cage to go back up to the top again. But I expect you realise what had happened! The two little boys, Jim and Basil, were nowhere to be seen. There was a big commotion now and everyone was darting here, there and everywhere to try and find them.

Jimini said to Jacko, "Come on, we're so small we can get into places where the grown-ups can't and who knows, we may discover where they are." Nanny told the Smarty Boys they must be careful and to remember where they were going so as not to get lost as well. Jimini and Jacko found one little tunnel, which was hidden from view. They wriggled down a crack in the wall and shone their torches ahead of them. These were small torches that Nanny had brought from Pen Onn and which they could hold in their hands.

They had to paddle through some pools of water and climb over some fallen rocks when suddenly they saw the two little boys, who were crying their eyes out. One of them had broken his leg when he clambered over the rocks and there was quite a lot of blood where they had scraped their knees. "Don't be frightened any more. We'll get help," said Jacko. Jimini ran back as fast as his little legs would take him while Jacko stayed with Jim and Basil, cheering them up with stories of Australia and his friends who lived there.

Before too long Jimini appeared with two officials carrying a stretcher. They hoisted Jim onto the stretcher and carefully took him back to the pit cage and into their first aid room back at the top. Everyone was cheering and Nanny and Grampy were very proud of their Smarty Boys.

It was decided that the Smartys should be rewarded, and to their amazement they were given a real boat so they could sail on a lake if they wanted and even go fishing, too. But that's another story. All I'm telling you now is that Grampy drove Nanny and the boys back to Pen Onn Cottage and to the delicious Knickerbocker Glories waiting in the fridge. All were tired and they were very glad to snuggle up in bed and dream of the day's adventures.

4

MONKEY BUSINESS

One day Jimini and Jacko asked Nanny if they could go to the zoo.

Well, Nanny doesn't like to see animals locked up in tiny cages but she knew of one zoo where the animals were kept in quite large compounds. She agreed that on the first fine day that came along she'd make some Welshcakes and peanut butter sandwiches, pull up some nice baby carrots from the garden, pick a few ripe tomatoes from the greenhouse and buy a bottle of lemonade. Then Grampy could drive them to the zoo.

As it happened the very next day was a fine one, so the Smarty Boys were up early, washed and dressed and pestering Nanny to be quick and get ready. After an hour or so everything was packed and off they set. It took two hours to get to the zoo, where Grampy paid for the tickets and in they went.

The first place they came to was the monkey house, and when Nanny's back was turned Jimini and Jacko climbed inside the bars and started mooching around. Of course being small, no one really noticed them – but a baby ape was lying on his back biting his toenails and wishing something exciting would happen. He saw Jimini and Jacko straight away and sat up in surprise, watching them curiously.

Suddenly he put out his paw and picked them up and pushed them up his nose!

Jimini and Jacko certainly hadn't expected this and it tickled inside his big nostrils until he sneezed them out again. The baby ape – his name was Snobby by the way – cupped the Smarty Boys in his paw and said in gibberish – although the Smartys could understand – who on earth are you two and where have you come from?

Jimini explained that they were friendly creatures on holiday in Wales, and that they had popped into the ape house just to have a bit of fun. Snobby said he'd teach them to swing from the branches of the trees and they all had a lovely time until Jimini and Jacko said they'd better move on and see some other animals. The last they saw of Snobby he was having a good telling off from his mother for telling fibs! You see, she wouldn't believe it when Snobby said he'd been playing with two little Smartys from Australia.

The next compound they came to contained two pandas. Now pandas love to eat bamboo shoots and they were dreamily munching away and having a happy time. Jimini and Jacko asked Nanny if they could go into the panda compound and she agreed, since they couldn't do much harm. Or so she thought. Jimini and Jacko picked up a bamboo shoot each and blew sidewards on the ends. It made a lovely musical note. They tried again and this time the sound was much louder and the two pandas heard it.

They trundled over to see what was happening and were not a bit worried to see the Smarty Boys. Now pandas are curious animals and they like to imitate, so they tried blowing sidewards on the ends of their bamboo shoots. Between the four of them they produced some really nice music and the elephants in the next compound heard it and started to blow bubbles with their trunks in a bath full of water.

This made a lovely gurgling sound and it was heard by the seals in the next compound. They started clapping their flippers together in a lovely slapping sound, which was heard by the African pigs in the next compound, who started to jump around squealing and snorting. Even the baby Welsh dragon picked up a rugby ball and started bouncing it around.

In next to no time the whole zoo was filled with every kind of animal sound you can imagine – some musical, some quite fearsome – just imagine the roaring of the lions for instance. The zookeepers didn't know how to deal with the situation but everyone could see that the animals were really enjoying it all. The zebras were running around in circles jumping over each other's backs, the penguins were popping out of the water and doing hand stands, while the polar bears were beating their huge paws on their tummies and pushing each other into their pool and laughing away.

All the children and parents who were visiting were marching in time to the music and the ice cream seller was so happy he started giving away cornets free of charge. This state of affairs went on for the best part of an hour until everyone was so tired they needed to stop for a rest. All the animals were saying in animal language – though Jimini and Jacko couldn't understand all of it – that this was the best day they'd had in all their lives and it was all because the Smarty Boys had come to see them.

When things had calmed down a bit, Jimini and Jacko came out of the panda compound and asked Nanny if they could eat their picnic down by the stream that ran through the zoo. So they all sat by the stream eating their lunch when all of a sudden something moved at the water's edge and who do you think popped out of the water? Perhaps you've guessed – if not I'll tell you – it was their old friend Stumpy, the sewer rat.

"You're a long way from home, aren't you?" asked Jacko. Stumpy replied that every now and again he liked a change from being in the sewer and loved to find a nice clean stream to swim in and have a good wash. When he realised the Smarty Boys were here on a visit he'd been hoping they'd come down to the water so he could say hello to them.

"As a matter of fact I've got a surprise for you," he said. "After I became the king of the rats I decided I'd better have a wife and I married the cutest little girl sewer rat you've ever seen. And now I've got a family of two boys and two girls." With that he gave a whistle and up popped the four baby rats and do you know, not one of them had a tail! But they didn't mind because no one made fun of them since they were now royal rats and children of the king. Even Nanny quite liked them and said they were very well brought up and most polite.

Well Nanny allowed Jimini and Jacko to play about and swim in the water until it was quite late. Then she called the boys and said it was time to pack up their leftovers and make their way home. It had been a tiring day and after a nice cup of hot chocolate, everyone snuggled down in bed to dream of zoos and pigs and Snobby the baby ape.

5

TO THE NORTH POLE!

One day when Jimini and Jacko were playing in the garden of Pen Onn Cottage, Stumpy appeared. "Hello, I've come out of the sewer for a bit of peace and for an adventure," he announced. "Any ideas, boys?" The Smarty Boys thought for a moment, then Jacko said in a low voice "I know – when Grampy isn't looking, let's take our rocket out of the garage and take Stumpy for a ride!"

"Ooh how exciting – I'll never ever have the chance to go up in a rocket unless you take me," said Stumpy. "Well, we'll have to plan things carefully," whispered Jimini, "so Nanny and Grampy don't suspect what we're up to."

Well first of all, the boys came into the kitchen and asked Nanny if they could pack a picnic because they'd like to play for the day in the field next to the garden. What a fib! Then they asked for their warm coats and their boots, in case it turned cold. Nanny thought this was a bit odd as it was quite a warm day, but she smiled and went to fetch their togs. Stumpy, by the way, had been sent home for his overcoat and some warm clothing, and was expected back in half an hour. So far, so good.

Next, they suggested to Grampy that he should take some garden rubbish down to the tip to get it out of Nanny's way. Grampy was always happy going to the tip so he loaded up the rubbish and called out to Nanny, "I think I'll have an hour in the library while I'm out and catch up on all the newspapers." Nanny was quite glad to have Grampy out from under her feet for a bit as she wanted to do some painting in the kitchen, and Grampy was doing some sawing there and making a lot of dust. Anyway, off went Grampy.

Now, when Nanny gets engrossed in something she tends not to notice what's going on around her, so she told the Smarty Boys to behave themselves in the field, and then promptly forgot about them. So Jimini, Jacko and Stumpy – who'd come back – quietly opened the garage door and wheeled out the rocket. They checked that the batteries were fully charged, inspected all the controls, climbed in, locked the doors and got ready for take-off.

Now when they had left Australia, their Dad had set all the controls to direct them straight on course for Pen Onn Cottage. Now, the Smartys weren't sure how to set a course in any other direction, so they fiddled about a bit and said "Oh well, it doesn't really matter where we go as long as we can get back again." Fortunately Jimini had the sense to make a note of the changes he had made to the dials so that he could reverse them in order to get safely back to Pen Onn again.

"Well, this is a pot luck trip so we must all put up with it," he said. "I've entered 4,000 miles into the mileage indicator, so let's see where we get to!" They checked their safety belts, then Jimini let off the brake and with a great gust of smoke, the rocket lifted off without any trouble. It sped up into the sky, flattened out after a while and then headed straight for the North Pole.

The three friends certainly hadn't expected to arrive there! But when the rocket touched down they were very glad to have brought their warm clothes along! They dressed quickly, opened the hatch and gingerly stepped out. Nothing was in sight but miles and miles of snow. At least, that's how it first seemed.

Jacko, who was always very quick to notice things, said "Look – there's something moving over there." The three friends trudged quietly in the direction Jacko had pointed out. Sure enough, there was someone there. It was a little Eskimo girl. She was crouched down peering into a hole in the snow, and in her hand she had a fishing line. She looked up when the boys approached and said in the most matter of fact way, "Hello you three, I'm Sheeba. What are your names?"

Introductions were made and everyone squatted down beside the hole in the snow. "What exactly are you doing?" asked Jacko. "Oh, just getting some fish for dinner," said Sheeba. "I may be small, but I learned to fish when I was just a toddler, so now my Mum and Dad send me out every morning to get fish for supper."

"Don't you have to pay for them?" asked Jacko. "Don't be silly," replied Sheeba, "if I catch some fish they're mine and they're free." Just then a big fish came along and started to pull on the bait at the end of her line. Quick as lightning, Sheeba yanked the fish out of the water and gave it a sharp tap on the head with a mallet she had at her side. The fish was dead instantly.

The Smarty Boys were thinking of the boat they'd been given at Big Pit, and thought it would be a good idea to learn how to fish, so they asked Sheeba if they could have a go. Jacko was the best at it. He landed two fish in next to no time. Jimini took a bit longer. But Stumpy didn't even want to try – he said fish made him come out in a rash so he wasn't going to risk getting anywhere near them.

"Come and see my pet polar bear," said Sheeba. The boys followed her back to the igloo where she lived and sure enough, there was a pure white polar bear hitched to a sleigh. "Jump in, everyone," cried Sheeba, "and Polo (that was the bear's name) will take us for a ride."

They all had to hang on very tightly because once he got started, Polo raced around like mad. Every now and again he did a somersault and the sleigh turned upside down too. The boys agreed it was great fun, though they soon started getting hungry and thinking about their peanut butter sandwiches. "I'd like to meet a few seals and perhaps a sea lion," said Jacko. "And I'd like to see a penguin," said Stumpy. "I've never seen one of those."

"Well I'd better get back for lunch now," said Sheeba. Everyone said goodbye and the boys made their way back to the rocket and tucked into their picnic. After lunch, they ventured out again and made their way in the opposite direction. Ahead of them, the snow was being churned about by the movement of some animal or other. Soon they could see what was going on.

Fifty-one penguins were having a snowball fight and having a lot of fun. The boys soon joined in, but sadly one snowball hit Stumpy in the eye, leaving it a bit sore. As you know, Stumpy was not the bravest of creatures and he soon wanted to go back to the rocket to rest. Jimini gave him the key and told him not to get lost or eat any more of the food on board.

The Smarty Boys went on and soon came across a lot of baby seals who were being taught how to swim by their mothers, next to a great big sea lion who was looking on. Jimini and Jacko were a bit afraid of Mumbo Jumbo the big sea lion, and by this time their toes were starting to get icy cold. They decided to get back to the rocket. Jimini reversed the instructions on the mileage dial and an hour later they were landing back in the garden of Pen Onn Cottage. Stumpy scooted off. Nanny had a lot to say about it all while Grampy, believe it or not, was still at the tip!

6

RESCUING A BADGER

It was St David's Day – the national day of Wales – and Nanny decided it was time for the two boys to see her dressed in her Welsh costume, complete with a tall black hat, colourful shawl and long skirt. She had a daffodil pinned to her top and looked splendid. Jimini and Jacko were very excited to be in Wales on such a special day, and knew there would be Welshcakes for tea later.

As it was springtime, Nanny noticed that the baby birds were being hatched. Some sparrows had built their nest under the roof tiles of Pen Onn Cottage, so it was no surprise when one day Grampy said that he could hear the babies chirping.

Whenever Nanny came out into the courtyard the parent birds made themselves scarce, but Jimini and Jacko were able to climb up on the roof as they pleased and go about almost unseen. So one morning they decided to visit a bird's nest to see what it was like there. They took the stepladder out of the garage and got up onto the roof, making their way along the gutters until they too could hear the chirping of the baby birds.

They crept under the roof tiles and almost immediately came across the nest. It was made of dried grass but woven in amongst the grass were interesting bits and pieces, such as all the fluff caught up in the washing machine that Nanny had thrown out after washing a red blanket. There was even an old hairnet of Nanny's! How the birds had got hold of this we shall never know, but it was lining the nest and looked very colourful.

Inside were five little scrawny baby birds. They hardly had a feather between them and were squabbling like mad. Each one wanted to be in the middle and as soon as one got into the middle, another one would peck it with its beak till it moved out. In short, the whole nest seemed to be on the move all the time. However when Jimini and Jacko appeared on the edge of the nest, everyone stopped quite still and said, "Look, here comes our dinner!"

"I think they mean us, Jimini. Let's get out of this quickly," said Jacko. The Smarty Boys scrambled down the ladder again and ran away as fast as they could into the field next to Nanny's garden. They kept on running past the cows, past the horses and past the sheep until they were out of breath. They dropped down onto the grass for a rest thinking what a narrow escape they'd had.

Just then they heard a rustling and some little grunting noises. Following the sounds, they found themselves near a hedge where the most awful sight met their eyes. There, tangled up in a lot of wire, was a fully-grown badger. "Whatever has happened?" asked Jacko. "I'm caught in a trap," gasped the badger. "I'm a mother badger, and I've been here all night. I've got five babies at home in my sett and they must all be dying for lack of milk. Please, please help me."

Jimini took charge of the situation as always. "Run back Jacko, and tell Nanny," he shouted. "She'll tell Grampy and he will know exactly what to do." Jacko did as he was told and relayed the message to Nanny. Grampy got on the phone straight away and phoned the

RSPCA. No answer. Next, Grampy rang the Wildlife Trust. No answer. Then Grampy phoned the Badger Conservation Trust. Immediately there was an answer and a kindly man said, "Tell us exactly where Pen Onn is and we'll be there within the hour."

Sure enough, he came bowling down the lane in his car not long afterwards. He had with him a big wire cutter and a wooden prong to hold the badger down while he tried to cut through the wires.

Everyone from the village of Pen Onn rushed across the field to where Jimini was waiting and trying to keep the poor mother badger calm. The man from the Badger Conservation Trust got to work straight away. It was very difficult to cut through the wires because the mother badger was terrified and could hardly keep still. At last he managed to disentangle the wires, and everyone stood back so that she could slip out of the trap and run away.

Before she did so, she whispered to the Smarty Boys – so no human could hear – "Climb up on my back and I'll take you to my sett and you can see my babies if they're still alive." Jimini and Jacko quickly did as they were told and off she galloped. Down the hillside and into the woods, past the broken tree, past the pond with the tadpoles in it and into the deepest part of the woods. Suddenly she stopped.

"Here we are," she announced, as she made her way down a hole in a grassy bank and into her sett. The five babies were there all right, but they were lying quite still and were cold to the touch. "Quick, run to the entrance of the sett and find all the leaves and moss you can to wrap around my babies," she said to Jimini. "They're still breathing but they need warming up."

Jimini and Jacko got to work. Out of nowhere, Stumpy had appeared and he was glad to help as well. No one spoke to one another, they just kept busy and rubbed the little bodies of the baby badgers and wrapped them up in moss. Gradually the little creatures began to get warm and one by one started to squeak and cry for their Mum. "Here I am darlings," she said, "come and have your milk." She lay down on her side and the five baby badgers quickly nuzzled in for their evening feed.

Stumpy said cheerio and went on his way. Jimini and Jacko stayed to tell the babies some bedtime stories about Australia and Pen Onn Cottage and Nanny's Welshcakes. "Does Nanny have slugs and snails in her garden?" asked one little badger. "Oh yes," said Jacko, "she's always grumbling about them." The badgers thought for a moment. "Well, tomorrow we'll all come over and have a feast of them and clear her garden at the same time" said one. "And if she makes some Welshcakes we'll stay on for tea as well."

They were as good as their word. Next day, Mother badger and her five babies appeared in Nanny's garden. It was a lovely warm day, so Nanny brought out some lemonade and everyone had a really good time eating slugs, snails and Welshcakes. Nanny and Grampy only fancied the cakes, of course. And Nanny promised to wear her Welsh outfit again soon.

7

A NAUGHTY DAY

I expect you've noticed that the Smarty Boys have been quite good and been very helpful to Nanny and other people since they arrived at Pen Onn Cottage, but now and again they go off the rails and are very naughty. They had one of those days not long after rescuing the badger, when the baby badgers came to call.

Jimini and Jacko were idling about in the garden obviously at a loose end, when over the wall came all the badgers one by one. As it happened, Stumpy came up from the sewer that day too, bringing with him his children – two boy rats and two girl rats, all without any tails. Nanny looked out of the window and shook her head in despair. "I can see it's going to be one of those days," she sighed. "Oh, let them get on with it," replied Grampy.

Outside in the garden, Jimini had lined up all the baby badgers and said, "Now, Jacko and I are going to teach you some naughty words. How would you like that?" The baby badgers started to giggle. "Oh, yes!" they chorused. "Right, then" said Jimini, "all say after me *Bums*". Everyone said *Bums*. The littlest badger could only say *Ums*.

"Now say *Piddle*," said Jimini. Everyone said *Piddle*. "Now say *Spit*." Everyone said *Spit*. "Now say *Tits*." Everyone said *Tits*. "And now say *Jumping Jackass*." Everyone said *Jumping Jackass*. "Now," said Jimini, "I want you all to think of a sentence that contains all of these words." One little badger said "Can *Tits* mean little birds as well as you-know-what? Because if so, this is my sentence." He took a deep breath and continued, "the Jumping Jackass put his bum in the piddle and then spit at the tits."

Everyone was laughing and rolling about because they thought this was very funny. "Now I've thought of one," said one of the baby rats. "The tits spit piddle on the Jumping Jackass." Again everyone screamed laughing. Just then Nanny came out into the garden. "Now stop this at once," she said sternly. "Those baby badgers will get into trouble when they get home and their mother will never let them come and play here again. Whatever must you be thinking of! Now go and play some other game please."

Nanny returned to making her Welshcakes, and Jimini and Jacko sat down to plan some other naughty things to do. Just then one of the baby badgers said he wanted to poo. "I know," said Jacko, "we'll all poo right in the middle of Nanny's lawn." "Do you think we should?" asked Stumpy. "After all, Nanny is very nice to us all." Jimini thought for a minute. "I say we've been good for long enough. This is going to be a naughty day – I can't help myself! We can be good again tomorrow."

So one by one, all the baby badgers and the baby rats, together with Stumpy and of course Jimini and Jacko, all pooed on Nanny's lawn. It was not a pretty sight I can tell you. Just then, Nanny came out to hang up her washing and when she saw what they'd done she was in a right temper.

"Go and fetch a shovel you baby badgers," she ordered. They were afraid to say No and trotted down to the greenhouse to fetch the shovel. Nanny turned to the baby rats. "Now, you go and fetch a plastic bag." They too did as they were told and scurried off to find a bag. "Now, Jimini and Jacko and Stumpy, since you're obviously the ringleaders you can shovel it all up," said Nanny firmly. Their faces fell, as they had imagined that Nanny would have found the poo much later and asked Grampy to clean it up. They took turns at shovelling it up and when they'd finished, Nanny said "Now, I'm bringing out an old tin bath with soap and water, and you can all wash your hands properly before anyone gets any lunch."

The bath of water was brought out onto the lawn by Grampy and everyone had a good wash. They all looked ashamed of themselves, though there was still a twinkle in the eyes of the Smarty Boys, so I wouldn't be surprised if they got up to something again after lunch. There was a hotchpotch of things to eat that day – peanut butter sandwiches, slugs and cream, snails and icecream, spiders with jam and sausages wrapped in leeks, with lemonade and Coke to follow. Plus of course Nanny's Welshcakes, which no one ever seemed to get fed up with.

After lunch all the animals were full up and very sleepy, so everyone curled up on the lawn for a snooze. Everyone, that is, except Jimini and Jacko. And this is the next naughty thing they did.

First they got some Sellotape and some cord from Grampy's study and made tails for all the rats from the cord, sticking one on the back end of each rat with the sticky tape. Then quietly and carefully, they tied everyone's tail to someone else's tail so all the rats and all the baby badgers were now joined together. An hour later the animals began to wake up and struggle to their feet, but no one could stand up straight. Each one thought the next one was playing a trick on them and soon all the animals were quarrelling with each other and making a huge hullaballoo.

Everyone was eventually untied and then Stumpy lined up his children, pulled off everyone's imitation tails and turned to the Smarty Boys. "Jimini and Jacko, you were my closest friends but this has hurt my feelings," he said in an offended voice. "I was born without a tail and I have become proud of that fact. But this has made a fool of me so I'm taking my family home and may not be back for some while – if ever – unless you say you're sorry."

Jimini and Jacko didn't want to say anything at first, but the badgers reasoned with them and eventually the two boys said together "We're very sorry for what we did, King Stumpy. We got carried away with being naughty but this won't happen again and we certainly didn't mean to make a fool of you."

Stumpy hesitated for a moment and then said, "Alright, everything's forgiven. You're once again my closest friends. However I must be getting back in case the sewer rats are getting up to mischief and need me to give a firm hand down there." Everyone shook hands and kissed the little girl rats, and then Stumpy and his family disappeared down a secret hole into the sewers of Pen Onn village.

Soon afterwards, Mother Badger climbed over the wall and started to line up her family. The smallest baby badger said "Mummy, I've learned lots of new words today." "Have you, my little darling?" said Mother Badger fondly. The baby badger thought for a moment and then announced, "Yes, I'd like to spit on tits and piddle on the bum of a Jackass." Mother Badger was speechless. She picked up the nearest twig she could find and shooed her babies back over the wall, threatening to give them a spanking.

"What a naughty thing to do," she told Jimini and Jacko. "My little badgers only knew words like please and thank you before today. Now I can see I'm going to have trouble with them." As an afterthought, she added, "however, I suppose children will be children all the world over and can't be good all the time." And then she gave the boys a little wink and disappeared over the wall. Jimini and Jacko smiled at each other. "It's been fun having a naughty day like this," said Jacko. "Now, let's go indoors and finish off those Welshcakes."

8
GOING FISHING

"Isn't it about time we took our boat out for a sail?" asked Jacko one day. Jimini asked Nanny if there were any lakes nearby where there would be fish to catch, and Nanny reminded them that the sea was only ten minutes away, so there were sure to be plenty of fish there.

The boat was soon loaded up on the back of Grampy's car and away they went to the sea. The weather was good, and the boys had several fishing lines and plenty of bait. When they got there Nanny decided that she and Grampy would have their lunch in the car by the water's edge while the boys went off to fish. Grampy had put some signal rockets in their boat and the boys knew that if they were in any trouble or wanted help of any kind, they simply had to send a signal rocket up and Grampy would send a rescue boat straight away.

It all seemed very straightforward. "Cheerio, Nanny" said the boys, "we'll be back with some fish for supper and perhaps you'll make us chips to go with them." Nanny nodded. "Have a good time and remember to be back by five o'clock sharp. It's two o'clock now, so let's set our watches and off you go."

The boys soon got the hang of steering their boat over the waves. They had hoisted the sail and soon the boat was merrily riding the waves and taking them out to sea. When they were about 300 yards offshore the sea became quite calm, so they pulled in the sail and dropped anchor. Next, as you can guess, they decided to have their picnic and only when they had finished did they drop their lines overboard and sit back to see what would happen. Both boys were rather sleepy after their lunch and with the sun shining down on them, they started to doze off.

Suddenly Jacko felt a mighty tug on his line. He jumped to his feet, waking Jimini in the process. But before he realised what was happening, he was pulled overboard. "Crikey," said Jimini, "I'd better jump in too just to see what's happening to Jacko." In he jumped – just in time to see poor Jacko being swallowed alive by a huge dogfish. At this moment – and what a good thing it was – Jimini realised he was able to swim underwater just like a fish. No one had ever realised before – as far as we know – that all Smarty Boys could swim like fishes.

Jimini followed the dogfish down to the seabed, where it lay down for a rest and went into a deep sleep. Jimini felt all along its sides until his hand came to a bump in its belly. He tapped on the side, put his mouth to its scales and shouted "Are you in there Jacko?" A faint sound came back, but it was only the fish's tummy rumbling. Jimini tried the same tactic on another bump he found. This time he was in luck. A frightened little voice answered, "Is that you, Jimini? Please find a way of getting me out soon or I'll drown in all the salt water and stuff inside this dogfish!"

"Now listen carefully," said Jimini. "I'm going to try the only trick I know. Nanny, bless her, put some pepper in our picnic box and I'm going to fetch it and sprinkle it under his nose. Hopefully he'll open his mouth to sneeze and you must be up there ready to make a quick getaway." Jacko was nearly in tears by this time. "I'll do my best," he promised. "Don't be long, Jimini!" His brother took charge of the situation once more. "Now, no feeling sorry for yourself. Just concentrate on climbing up to the fish's mouth and keep your chin up. I've never failed you yet have I?"

With that speech behind him, Jimini swam up to the surface again and jumped back into the boat. I'm afraid he forgot all about the rocket signals, but he knew he had to be very quick before the dogfish woke up and swam away. He put the pepper pot in his pocket and was soon back on the seabed. Thank goodness the dogfish was still there. Jimini sprinkled pepper all over its face but amazingly it didn't have any effect. Goodness, what am I going to do next, he wondered.

Just then a friendly herring was passing by and noticed what was going on. "Pepper isn't any good," he told Jimini. "The only way to make a dogfish sneeze is by putting a Welshcake under its nose. They hate Welshcakes 'cos they always give the dogfish a sneezing fit."

Jimini remembered that Nanny had put some freshly baked Welshcakes in their lunchbox, so he swam up to the surface again and jumped back in the boat. He soon found the Welshcakes and dived to the bottom again. The dogfish was just beginning to stir after its nap. Quickly Jimini held three Welshcakes right under its nose. Anyone would think the dogfish had been shot! First it went rigid, then it went limp, then it opened its mouth and gave the most almighty sneeze. Out of its mouth shot all the contents of its stomach, including poor little Jacko.

Jimini grabbed him and swam back to the surface again with Jacko holding on to his T-shirt for dear life. The boys leapt over the side of the boat and collapsed spluttering on the deck. "Let's have a look at you to see if you're hurt in any way," said Jimini. Jacko seemed none the worse for his adventure except in one respect. Everyone has special juices in their stomach to digest and break down the food they eat. Some of these juices can be quite acid and quite strong. Well, the digestive juices of the dogfish had turned Jacko's hair a bright orange colour, and I'm afraid Jimini couldn't help but laugh. Jacko was a bit offended but he said "Well, at least I'll never forget the day I was swallowed by a dogfish and everyone will have to believe me when they see my hair!"

Well after this terrifying adventure, the Smarty Boys didn't have much strength to carry on fishing so they decided to get back to shore again. They hoisted the sail, madly waved the Welsh flag Grampy had given them in case they got into trouble, and were just about to pull up the anchor when they realised there was a big salmon on the end of Jimini's line. Quick as a flash, they pulled the salmon on board, killed it instantly with their mallet just as Sheeba had shown them (you remember, the little Eskimo girl at the North Pole?) and steered triumphantly back to the beach.

Nanny couldn't believe her eyes when she saw the salmon and almost fainted when she saw Jacko's orange hair. "You must wait till we get home to hear the full story," said Jimini. "It's a real adventure this time, Nanny. Everyone will be surprised and I bet no one will believe us!"

9

MEETING AN OCTOPUS

Jimini and Jacko's adventure in the water didn't stop them from wanting to go out in their boat again. They had learned a lot about safety from their last trip, so on the next fine day they asked Nanny if they could go back out to sea. Nanny and Grampy took them back to the coast and watched as they launched the boat, hoisted the sail and made their way out again into calm waters. They had their signal rockets on board, as well as a picnic box and some Welshcakes, just in case they had more trouble with a sly dogfish.

This time, they had also brought wetsuits, goggles and proper diving gear, so they could go exploring underwater. Of course, as I mentioned before, the Smarty Boys had discovered they could swim like fishes and breathe for some considerable time underwater without coming up for air. They liked the idea of swimming underwater and it made them feel very important.

Soon they dropped anchor, put on their togs and slipped over the side of the boat into the cold, blue-green water. They swam for a time side by side just enjoying the experience and admiring all the different kinds of fish and sea creatures that were around. They saw one dogfish eyeing them suspiciously, and wondered if it was the same one that had swallowed Jacko. Needless to say they didn't hang about to find out!

They swam around the rocks and in amongst the starfish when Jacko, who as you know was always quick to notice things, said "Gosh, that looks like a sunken boat over there!" And indeed, about 30 yards away a big dark object was lying on the seabed. "Approach with care," Jimini warned. (I had forgotten to say that the boys were both carrying small microphones that enabled them to talk to each other underwater).

The boys swam towards the dark object while staying close to each other and keeping a wary eye open for sea monsters. Sure enough, lying on the seabed was a boat. It wasn't a liner or anything like that, but it had a cabin and was quite sizeable. It had obviously been there for some time as there was quite a lot of rust on it and some parts were completely rotted through. Jimini managed to open the cabin door, which they carefully wedged open so they could slip out easily again if necessary, and in they went.

There were bits and pieces lying around everywhere – a few cups and a kettle for example, and several tins of jam and baked beans. There was some cutlery, including a big breadknife, and on the floor sticking out of a cupboard was a biggish black box. Jacko pulled up the hinged lid and his heart stopped beating for an instant. "I think we've found buried treasure," he squeaked excitedly. Jimini took charge.

"Let me see what's there," he said. Inside the box were handfuls and handfuls of coins – possibly even gold, he thought. "Well," he said sounding superior, "if this is buried treasure let's tell no one. This could make Nanny's fortune and she'll be able to come and see us when we're back in Australia. If there's any over she can buy a new car, and we both need haircuts, too."

The two boys struggled to carry the treasure chest back out of the cabin door and on to the broken down deck of the ship. "Let's have a breather," said Jacko. The words were barely out of his mouth when he suddenly saw Jimini yanked off his feet and swung right across the bow of the boat. Although he was trying to stay calm, Jimini yelled, "Jacko, this is a serious situation – I've been caught in the tentacles of an octopus and he's squeezing the life out of me. Be quick and get back inside the cabin, fetch the breadknife and do your very best to cut me free!"

For a moment Jacko was paralysed. But he soon recovered and swam back into the cabin, found the breadknife and raced outside again. Jimini was practically on his last legs. This is touch and go, thought Jacko. Taking an almighty swipe, he brought the knife down on the huge tentacle of the octopus. It had no effect. He tried again but still no effect. Just as he was about to try once more a familiar voice behind him said, "All you've got to do is dangle a Welshcake in front of the octopus, silly!"

Jacko turned to find the friendly herring passing by. How lucky they were to have brought the Welshcakes with them! Jacko took one out of his pocket and bravely approached the octopus. It worked like magic. The octopus gave a squeal of horror and released Jimini in an instant, dropping him like a broken doll on the deck.

He must be dead, thought Jacko, and big tears welled up in his eyes. He had always thought Jimini would be there for him forever. He stroked Jimini's hair and rocked him back and fro. A muffled voice suddenly cried, "for goodness sake Jacko, don't be such a baby! A cuddle now and again is OK but now is not the time. I need a doctor! Get me back to Nanny and she'll know what to do."

Jacko managed to swim back to their boat, dragging the injured Jimini along with him. He didn't forget the treasure chest, either. He pushed Jimini and the treasure chest up over the side of the boat and then clambered aboard. Then he pulled up the anchor, hoisted the sail once more and steered back to shore. Luckily Nanny and Grampy had guessed something was wrong after such a long time and were on the alert looking out for them.

Grampy took one look at the injured Jimini and said, "This boy needs to see a doctor as soon as possible. On second thoughts, he's not really human, so perhaps we'd better take him to a vet." And that's exactly where the boys were taken. All the dogs and cats in the vet's surgery looked on with great interest and all their owners said Jimini must go in straight away without waiting his turn.

The vet pulled and probed, and decided to take an X-ray. "Lungs OK, heart fine and no broken bones," he pronounced. "I think the biggest trouble is that I can see his tummy's empty – so he's probably dying of hunger rather than any injury. I'd better give him an injection to be on the safe side though." At the very mention of an injection, Jimini shot upright and announced, "No need for that – I'm feeling fine!"

"No getting out of this my lad," said the vet. "Let's have your bottom." Jacko felt very sorry for Jimini at this point and said, "Look, if it makes you feel any better I'll have an injection as well." Jimini perked up no end at this and they both had a needle in their bottoms and were surprised to find they didn't feel it one bit.

Nanny paid the vet his fee and they all made their way home to Pen Onn Cottage. When Grampy was stowing the boat away in the garage he noticed the treasure chest. "What's this?" he asked. The boys chorused "We think there's a fortune in gold coins, so you and Nanny can have it for being such good grandparents."

Well, I wish I could tell you that all the coins were real gold. As it happened they were just token money coins from a children's board game and had no value at all. No one minded, however. Everyone was just glad to have Jimini out of danger and both boys safely back home. "Let's put the kettle on," said Grampy. "We all deserve a cuppa."

10

SAVING STUMPY

"Well, Nanny," said Jimini one day, "we'll soon be going back to Australia you know. Our holiday is nearly over and it will soon be time for us to leave Wales." Nanny thought for a moment. "Well, you'd better be saying goodbye to all your animal friends. You've only got time for one more adventure so perhaps you'd better call for Stumpy and take him over to the wild wood to see the badger family."

"Good idea," said Jacko. "We'll do that this morning." The boys went out into the garden and found a hole in the wall through which Stumpy had disappeared and shouted down "King Stumpy! Woo-hoo!" They didn't get any answer so they wriggled down the hole and found themselves in a kind of passageway. It was very dark and a bit spooky, so they nipped back quickly and borrowed a torch from Grampy. He put a new battery in, so they would have light for a long time, and back they went into the hole in the wall.

It seemed ages before they could find any sign of the sewer rats and when they did, unfortunately it was dead one. A little later they came across another dead rat and it was clear that something was terribly wrong down there. "Stumpy, Stumpy!" they called for the umpteenth time. At last there was a faint reply. "Over here, past the bend in the pipe," said the voice.

When the boys got round the bend, a sorry sight met them. Most of the rats were lying down on their backs, panting and whimpering. Stumpy was there and seemed to be all right although he looked terribly tired. "Whatever is the trouble?" asked Jacko. "I really don't know. Most of the rats became ill three days ago, and more are falling ill every day," said Stumpy. "I'm alright but my wife is ill and so are my two boys."

Jimini could see he'd have to take command here and said in a firm voice, "I know a little about medicine as Jacko and I have had a few things wrong with us in the past. Let's bring one of the rats over here into the light so we can do a proper examination." Stumpy brought over his wife Popsy and laid her gently in front of Jimini so they could shine the torch brightly on her. Jimini carefully examined her eyes and her tummy and between her toes. "I'm pretty sure," he said at last, "that all the rats have got athlete's foot. It's pretty common in humans but it only affects them between the toes. It's not serious, just a nuisance, but in rats it can be fatal."

"Do you mean it could wipe us all out?" asked Stumpy. "'Fraid so," said Jimini, "unless we can get some treatment for you straightaway. Jacko, make your way back to Pen Onn Cottage. You'll have to go without the torch – I'll need it here. I've got the feeling Grampy had athlete's foot not so long ago and it's likely that he's got some lotion and powder left over. Bring it back with any tablets that Nanny thinks will be useful." Jacko went off as bravely as he could as he knew he'd have to pass the two dead rats on the way, and he could hardly see a thing in the dark.

Next, Jimini turned to Stumpy. "Go and find every rat in the sewer and line them all up," he said. "The ones who are still fit must help to carry all the invalids." Stumpy looked doubtful. "I'm afraid things are pretty unhygienic down here," he explained. Jimini looked around. "I'm sorry to be critical, but the worker rats are not doing their jobs very well," he told Stumpy. "The place must be swept and hosed down and everyone must stay together to have their treatment. Jacko's been gone now for half an hour, so he can't be much longer."

Jacko had made his way past the two dead rats, up the long tunnel and back to Pen Onn Cottage. I bet you can guess what Nanny was doing. But she sat down for a moment and listened to the tale Jacko had to tell. "My word, what a pickle they're in," she said. "Now, let's pack a bag. Here's the athlete's foot lotion. Every rat must have their necks rubbed with it. Next, the powder. Every rat must be sprinkled with it. Now, in this bottle is a mixture of cough medicine and cod liver oil. Every rat must take half a teaspoon. You can take my special Welsh lovespoons to help measure it out. Finally, in this bag are some fresh Welshcakes. Every rat must eat a half. If that doesn't cure them, nothing more can be done."

Jacko found it quite difficult to cart all these things back down the narrow passage, but Grampy had given him another torch, which made the going easier. Eventually he got back down to the bend in the pipe where he'd left Jimini and Stumpy. All the rats were lined up on their feet or lying in neat rows.

Jacko carefully repeated Nanny's instructions and Jimini said "Stumpy, stand here. As each rat comes past or brings a sick rat along, you must rub each one with this lotion around their neck. Jacko, stand on this stone. As each rat passes you, sprinkle the powder over them. When they come past me I'll give everyone a dose of medicine and then each one must eat half a Welshcake. As long as we're careful, no one will be left out."

Well the whole process took quite a long time, but eventually every single rat, including Stumpy, had been given the four treatments. Nanny had said that if it was to do any good, they would see signs of it in an hour's time. It seemed ages before an hour had passed and then suddenly, one by one, all the sewer rats were violently sick. They seemed to be getting worse rather than better, and what a mess they made! Good job it was in the sewer and everything could all be washed away in the pipes.

After this, the rats were soon on the mend and King Stumpy couldn't stop shaking the hands of Jimini and Jacko and telling them they were heroes. "We'd never have got better if you hadn't come down the sewer to say goodbye," he cried. All the rats cheered, Stumpy gave them both a hug and the boys climbed back up the passageway to Pen Onn Cottage to tell Nanny and Grampy about their final big adventure.

11

MAKING WELSHCAKES

Welshcakes – Jimini and Jacko's favourite treat – were traditionally made on an old fashioned bakestone, but they're easy to make using either a cast iron griddle or frying pan. Don't use a lightweight non-stick frying pan as you don't want them to burn!

Ingredients

225g self-raising flour

75g caster sugar

100g butter, cut into small pieces

½ tsp mixed spice

50g currants

1 egg

1-2 tbsp milk

Pinch of salt

Five easy steps

1 - Tip the flour, butter, sugar, mixed spice and salt into a large mixing bowl, rubbing the ingredients together with your fingers till you have a crumbly mixture. Stir in the currants.

2 – Add the egg with the milk and work this into the flour mixture. You should end up with a nicely firm dough that can be rolled out easily on a lightly floured board. Aim to get it around 1/4 inch (5mm) thick.

3 – Use a 6cm pastry cutter to cut out the cakes, then grease the griddle or frying pan with a little butter, heating it until the butter bubbles slightly.

4 – Cook your Welshcakes for roughly 3-4 minutes each side, till they are golden brown, crisp and slightly risen.

5 – Now sprinkle them with a little caster sugar and ideally serve them while still warm. Delicious! They are also a treat with butter and jam.

The Welshcakes will keep for up to a week in an airtight tin. Even baby dragons are known to love them!

12

ON OUR WAY...

Dear Nanny and Grampy,

We're sorry to say that we have decided to leave Pen Onn. This will be a shock to you. You've been wonderful to us and put up with all our naughty antics. But we miss seeing children our own age. Before we go back home we are going to look for new adventures with a family in another part of the world – maybe Canada.

We'll drop in to see you again when we're on our travels, and hope you understand. We told all our animal friends at Pen Onn some time ago and they all cried but said we must go off to see the world.

We know we shall never have Welshcakes like yours again!

Lots of love

Jimini and Jacko xx

Artist and graphic designer Hafsa Pinar, who lives and works in Turkey, has numerous children's books to her credit. A highly acclaimed and self-taught illustrator, she loves bringing characters to life in both print and digital formats.